The Eye and the Sausage
& Other Stories

* * *

DOUGLAS RAMSAY

Food for Thought – Enjoy

Douglas Ramsay

First published in 2023 by Tors House Publishing

Publishing services provided by Lumphanan Press
www.lumphananpress.co.uk

Front cover artwork by Annie Grant
www.artbyanniegrant.com

ISBN: 978-1-3999-4820-3

Printed & bound by Imprint Digital, UK

Contents

The Eye and the Sausage

WHAT A WEDDING, WHAT A stooshie; the inside story of the recent event where two families fell out over festive food of all things, was recounted to me by my friend Luther. I was curious because the story had been reported in some of the newspapers.

Luther recalled the event. Edward, or 'Big Ed' as he's called, is a distant nephew of mine and was to be married to a girl called Angela who belonged to a family of strict vegetarians. My family are all hearty meat-eaters so there is bound to be some tension between us and them. Angela herself is a sensible girl and often shared a hamburger with Big Ed when her family were not around. The pair of them were deeply in love.

The wedding reception was held in a glitzy hotel with two long tables on opposite sides of a large hall. One table was for the meat-eaters, the other for the vegetarians in case the servings of food became mixed up. The top table, facing the guests, was of course mixed with the bride and groom and the immediate family.

Despite the rather brittle atmosphere, all went well until a delicious starter was served. The trouble started when the best man chose the famous words of Robert Burns for the grace. He only got as far as the third line, 'But we hae meat and we can eat,' when one of the bride's more belligerent guests, a pale and slightly jaundiced youth with advanced vitamin B12 deficiency, shouted, "NOT ALL OF US!" and threw a leg of broccoli at the opposite table where it added to the hair adornment of one of the bridesmaids.

A slice of black pudding came flying across the other way and the wedding dinner degenerated into a food fight between the two tables while the top table looked on in horror and tried to stop the fight which both factions seemed to enjoy. The melee only came to a halt when one of the vegans was hit in the eye and injured by a flying sausage.

The hotel management had, by now, called the police. Statements were taken but the groom's family treated the investigation light-heartedly ... too light-heartedly. "If the sausage had hit someone in the eye, it must have been a wee willie winky sausage," said one witness. Another, fancying himself as a philosopher, said that no one was to blame. "If pigs have wings, then sausages can fly," he announced – misquoting an old saying. The alleged culprit denied causing the injury saying that he had thrown a curled sausage which he had seen returning like a boomerang before it reached the other table.

"Like the curled variety which almost caused a revolution in Kurdistan when a visitor likened the national delicacy to a horse's bushwhacker?" I suggested.

"Something like that." Luther continued with his story. The proceedings degenerated into complete farce when the victim demanded a swab be taken from his eye to confirm the presence of sausage DNA, and after the police left, the happy event was enveloped in a pall of gloom which continued during the rest of the meal.

But the groom was made of sterner material and after a lengthy period, he rose to his feet. "If no-one is going to congratulate the bride and groom," he announced, "I will offer the toast to my lovely bride and the groom myself." He made a splendid job of it, soothing both factions and the next day, the newlyweds left for an unforgettable honeymoon in Kurdistan. They now have a healthy two year old thriving on broccoli and hamburgers.

"What happened to the culprit who threw the sausage?" I asked.

"The eye injury settled with no lasting effects," replied Luther. "The Fiscal Office decided not to proceed with the case. They said it would bring the Court into disrepute."

"That was very wise." I observed. "One just has to imagine learned Counsel arguing over the significance of sausage DNA."

My Life as a Sweetie Paper

How did it come to this? I'm here in the gutter, wet and cold with streams of water running over me and filthy dirty car tyres hissing past only a few feet away every few seconds. What a miserable predicament to be landed in! It wasn't always like this: I was born in a state-of-the-art modern factory, printed with enticing letters and wrapped with a delicate lining of silver foil round a bar of delicious chocolate. No silver lining here in the gutter though. Brooding on this, I scarcely noticed that a plastic bag had been borne by the wind and had lodged next to me in the gutter. His cheerful message had been foreshortened.

"Eve Helps," I read. "Hullo Eve," I said, "who do you help?"

"I can't help anyone in my present state," replied the carrier bag. "Someone put a cucumber inside me, and I have lost most of my message to the public. It should be 'Every Little Helps.'"

"I sympathise, plastic carrier bags are not made to last nowadays, and cucumbers are often the main villains causing bursts and tears."

The carrier bag looked thoughtful and then went into a soulful monologue ... "Rip goes the carrier and life goes on. Every moment, every hour, every day leads us further from our dreams of being the most important carrier bag in the business to ... "

"Hey!" I interrupted, "that speech is not original. It's been taken from the first page of a famous English novel."

"Well, at least, the key words have been changed," replied the carrier bag. He paused for a moment or two. "Look behind you," he went on, "there's a dog approaching and he's interested in you."

I felt threatened. A wet inquisitive nose was just above me and next to it was a dangerous set of teeth which could further tear me apart.

"He's looking for a taste of chocolate," said the carrier bag. "It could be worse if it were the other end just above you."

"At least the other end does not have teeth," I replied as the slavering jaws approached. I wished that I was a tooth fairy or better still, an anti-tooth fairy with a magic wand as the Hound of the Baskervilles stretched his tail out from the kerb to get his face in position above me in the gutter.

Suddenly, a car roared out of nowhere close to the kerb and ran straight over the dog's tail which was stretched out over the road. Pluto gave a screeching bark and went howling off into the distance followed by his owner cursing and calling his name.

"Did you see that?" said the carrier. "That was a learner driver taking her driving test in the car."

"A wonderful driver," I replied. "I just hope she passes her test."

"I doubt it," said the carrier bag sadly. "Examiners don't like it when a driver goes too near the kerb. She would certainly have failed if she had hit the kerb."

"Well, she did not hit the kerb."

"There's a gust of wind coming," said the carrier. "I'm off," and he danced away in the breeze like a director's nostalgic touch in an arty film. I watched him go, lazily following the wind coils and his message changing from 'Eve helps' to 'Every Little Helps' and finally to 'Ever yelps' as he suddenly flew up in the air. I turned my attention to a two-page section of a newspaper which had landed next to me in the gutter.

The paper gradually unfolded, and a picture emerged so that I could see that it was a photograph of someone giving a talk. "That's our president," said the newspaper proudly. "He is announcing that wind power has just come of age and is producing one hundred per cent of the electricity for the grid in our beloved country."

"I'd have thought it would have been announced on television first."

"It was to have been on TV first but there were four power cuts yesterday, the last two scuppering the broadcast."

"Very embarrassing for him."

"Well, not really, he's used to it and it was not cold enough for him to have to don his overcoat."

The wind was getting playful again: a sustained breeze started to curl up the newspaper sheets so that an advert for the Essex House Hotel became the 'sex House' and the photo of the president regressed as the pages blew away down the gutter in the wake of the carrier bag.

"I wish I could follow them," I thought. "It might dry me out a bit." I was stuck fast, however, in this same miserable part of the gutter. The wind was really getting up now and a fresh shower of rain added to my discomfort. Suddenly a large cardboard box, thrown from a white van, landed with a thump and almost on top of me.

"Sorry," said the box. "Not my fault though. Someone just threw me here."

"A pretty large box to throw onto a busy road though," I ventured.

"Not as large as one of my brothers," replied the box. "He was thrown onto a reasonably quiet street in a housing estate and attracted the attention of a two-year-old toddler who thought it would be grand to put the box over his head and move about under it. The little brat eventually moved out into the road and sat under the box. The next thing that happened: a learner driver with an instructor came barging along the street towards him."

"Sounds ominous: what happened?"

"The driver thought he could run into the box and knock it out of the way, but the instructor told him no. Someone might have put a load of bricks in it as a joke. He said that he would stop and move it into the side rather than going round it."

"So, what happened?"

"He picked the box up and discovered the small child crouching underneath and laughing at being discovered."

"I don't suppose he laughed."

"No, he was furious and took the child across the road to a small group of adults on the other side of the road and started berating them for putting the toddler in danger."

"I'll bet they were sorry."

"Not at all: they said the child did not belong to any of them and that they had not seen him playing with the cardboard box."

"So, what happened then?"

"He left the child in the care of the adults who were now as concerned as he was and made off just as a young woman appeared on the street shrieking for her kiddie."

"A voice was heard in lamentation,
Rachel weeping for her children," recited the box.

Time passed. Someone came along the road and kicked the box to pieces along the pavement. The rain became heavier, and I was almost submerged under a dirty stream of water when a gigantic hand reached down, plucked me from the gutter and held me as far as possible from himself with two fingers. I was taken up a long driveway and tossed unceremoniously into a large, blue plastic bin among various pieces of paper, metal cans and plastic containers. "Ah good." I said to myself, "a recycling bin no doubt. At least, it is warm and dry in here and I am to be recycled into another life. Perhaps I will be made into the page of a learned book or even into a copy of a famous declaration of statehood."

In the meantime, I had plenty of company, the pieces of plastic were happy to chat away and the polystyrene blocks, which should not have been in the bin, were very knowledgeable since they had been round pieces of electronic equipment. Yes, life was definitely looking up with the promise of things to come.

Of Love, Crocodiles and the Orient Express

SOME ACTION WAS NEEDED HERE: on several occasions recently, I had noticed an unlikely couple of strangers at the top of my garden, sitting half hidden under an apple tree by a pond I was constructing. The young woman and her perky little sister presumably thought I was at work and were making hay while the late winter sun shone.

An idea occurred to me. I took two steaming cups of coffee and crept up the garden to surprise them.

"Coffee is served," I announced.

The young woman backed away with the child hiding behind her skirt. "I'm sorry," she said, "I meant no harm."

"Well, sit down." I motioned to the garden seat. "You do have the loveliest of voices."

She told me her name was Aline and her young sister, aged five, was called Alice. Both were trying to escape the noise on the other side of the garden, and I told Aline that they could sit here if they wanted but she should not allow Alice to come alone because of the pond.

"She's uncertain about your stone crocodile," said Aline. "Can you reassure her?"

I took Alice up to the pond and told her, "He's a good crocodile. He guards the frogs and tadpoles from the birds."

"Why does he not frighten the tadpoles?" asked Alice.

"When he looks up, he is snappy and when he looks down, he is happy." I replied.

She gave a high-pitched squeal of laughter and the next day, I noticed a garland of wild flowers and pondweed around the crocodile's head.

In the following weeks, I gradually came to know Aline and her young sister. She told me rather pointedly that she had a boyfriend, Walter, whom she intended to marry in the autumn. They had met on the internet, and he was presently in Lagos setting up a business in which they were both investing. I told her, as convincingly as I could, that I had recently broken up a relationship and was not looking for another at present. However, we found that we had many shared interests: Aline liked reading widely and even enjoyed the classical novels of science fiction which I liked. She told me one day about a particularly haunting scene from John Wyndham's novel *The Chrysalids* where the young boy, in a post nuclear world, accidentally discovers that his playmate, Sophie, has six toes on one foot and is sworn to silence lest the young girl and her family are expelled from the community.

Foreign travel was another source of mutual interest and, at one meeting where I felt slightly bold, I told her that I'd had a curious dream that both of us were celebrating our ruby wedding on the Orient Express and our grandchildren were entertaining our fellow passengers. "I don't believe a word of it," she said blushing slightly and we both laughed it off.

Little Alice was more direct. She told me that next week was her birthday and she wondered if I was going to give her a present. I bought her the book *Alice in Wonderland* which she peered at suspiciously as I read it to her. She was beginning to lose interest when I came to the point where Alice started falling after going down the rabbit hole.

She piped up. "Why did she go in after the rabbit if she was going to fall? She should have waited for the rabbit to come back out again." Alice laughed and ran off to her favourite place at the hedgerow.

One evening, Aline's parents invited me to dinner. I met her elder brother for the first time. He was married with a small family and made a great fuss of Alice. His relationship with Aline seemed slightly strained however and he did not mention her boyfriend. Aline was alone next time she came into the garden, and I missed seeing Alice. "She has a nasty cold," Aline told me and the next time I saw the little girl she looked pale and moody. I suggested to Aline that we take her to the seaside to cheer her up.

Aline reluctantly agreed and was relaxed and chatty on the beach. Alice, now fully recovered, played happily beside us on the sand or pulled me down to the water's edge to paddle in the sea. She shrieked with excitement as the occasional wave broke over her knees and soaked the hem of her floral print dress. In the evening, she lay asleep on her sister's lap in the back of the car and I had not the heart to tell them to use their seat belts properly. This was the high point of our relationship. The next time I saw Aline, she told me her boyfriend was returning and she would have to distance herself from me. Alice, however, was a solace and a joy. She came up to me and placing both elbows on my knee, fixed her abyssal dark grey eyes on my face. "Why don't you marry Aline?" she demanded. "Then I could keep coming into your garden and see my crocodile."

Aline heard her but said nothing. After that, the two sisters came less frequently, and I felt the chill wind of impending change. One day, in late July, I found Aline sitting despondent on the garden seat. Her eyes were slightly swollen on her delicate heart shaped face and she had used extra eye shadow to cover this. "I have an allergy," she told me. I went over to Alice who was sitting on the crocodile's head staring moodily into the pond and running her fingers through her hair. "Alice," I said, "Your big sister looks sad."

"He's left her," she said angrily. "He's taken all her money. He's a bad man."

I took Alice's hand. "What can we do?" I asked.

"Why don't you go over and kiss her and make her better?"

"Thank you, Alice," I murmured, "you are a wonderful child." I bent to kiss the top of her head. Her hair had the fragrance of childhood innocence, orange blossom and a liberal dose of pond water. "Don't do that!" she shrieked squirming away "You're supposed to kiss Aline, not me." God she was in a bad mood this morning.

Chastened, I went back to Aline and sat beside her. "You've been hurt, Aline. I'm so sorry." I clasped her hand.

"I'll be OK," she said quietly but I watched fascinated as a tear formed on her cheek at the end of a trail of eyeshadow, a glistening jewel in the midday sun. On impulse, I gently kissed her cheek. "I don't know if you should do that?" she murmured but her hand tightened on mine.

"Why not?" I replied. "I'm in love with you Aline. Leave a tear but on your cheek and I'll not look for wine. I want to take Alice's advice and marry you."

"Oh, you and your misquotes." She paused. "Before you say anything else, I have something I must tell you." Another pause, then she went on. "Alice is not my sister, she's my child. That is partly why Walter left me."

"I guessed that long ago and it matters not. Your wedding gift would be the most precious a man can receive, a little daughter to love and cherish." I hoped I did not sound too arcane.

"And spoil rotten?" Aline tried to smile but she became serious again. "There's more." The words would not come out, so I told her to put her arms round my neck and whisper in my ear. I felt myself drowning in her delicious feminine fragrance as she did this. I was taken aback by what she told me, and many things now became clear. Just now however, she needed words to comfort her. "Aline," I said. "You were very young at the time and Alice is a healthy, happy child. There is nothing wrong with her and she has five beautiful toes on each foot. What else can I say to reassure you?"

Aline thought for a moment. "Will you still take me on the Orient Express?"

"Yes Aline, I promise you I will take you on the Orient Express."
"And Alice?"

"I would not go without her," I replied and she rested her head on my shoulder. We both sat in a silence which bonded rather than separated us. There would be problems in the future but with good sense, good faith and good humour these would be ignored or over-come. This was a moment to savour and fix in my mind forever. My reverie was abruptly disturbed: a small soaking wet hand clutched my sleeve. "Come quick!" Alice pleaded. "The crocodile's fallen into the pond and is drowning."

"Crocodiles don't drown," I started to say but I was dragged unceremoniously off the garden seat and, together, Alice and I went to rescue Mr Crocodile from the pond.

The Iceberg's Lament

To melt or not to melt: that is the question. Am I now a South Sea Island or still just an iceberg? Let me explain: the trouble started over one hundred years ago when I was floating in the North Atlantic with an unusually large number of fellow icebergs. It was bad luck that I was the one to be hit by the *Titanic* which was steaming full speed ahead without looking where it was going or heeding the dangerous conditions of ice in the seas. Perhaps everyone was busy with the arrangement of the deckchairs for the following day.

My damage was slight, but the liner sank in a perfectly calm sea. A number of factors for worldwide and continued publicity were present. Important passengers were on board and there were not enough lifeboats for all passengers. Also, the ship was considered to be unsinkable and nearby ships ignored repeated distress signals. The long and short of it was that I received a torrent of bad publicity though I was in no way to blame. Any insurance company will tell you that if a vehicle travelling at speed and not paying attention, crashes into something which has a perfect right to be there, that vehicle is wholly at fault. My insurance company, 'Icelandic Properties PLC' absolved me of all blame but someone had taken a photograph of me, a colossal mass of ice towering over the stricken vessel and things looked very bad for me. Someone even wanted to call me *Icy McIceface* but, fortunately, the name never stuck. I was however given the cold shoulder by my fellow icebergs, and as the bad publicity continued to grow, I was advised to leave the North Atlantic.

It was with a heavy heart that I floated south across the equator, losing a great deal of weight on the way but much of it was regained as I made it to the waters around the South Pole. A visit by a troop of penguins was a welcome diversion at one point. They were much nicer than the clumsy polar bears who used to lumber over me way up north. I was also glad I had not carried any of these bears to the Antarctic. This would have created an ecological disaster to add to my woes.

After many years, I reached the South Sea Islands and decided to settle there and disguise myself as one of these delightful little places. Over the years, I covered myself with soot, volcanic ash and seagull droppings and, eventually, I was accepted by my fellow islands though they did sometimes wonder how I could move around so easily. I was also visited by the South Sea Islanders, who were delightful people, but they had to devise new dances to keep them on their toes and prevent frostbite.

In 2012, there was a resurgence of interest worldwide in the *Titanic* as the centenary of its sinking was celebrated. I kept as low a profile as possible: I did not want hordes of souvenir hunters swarming over me and chipping off chunks of ice which would be sold at a hundred dollars per kilogram on the black market. Fortunately, I was not recognised.

What of the future? I will eventually melt away and if boatloads of tourists keep swarming over me, eating salt and vinegar crisps and throwing their empty packets down, I doubt if I will last another hundred years. I will eventually become a layer of scum and ashes in the sea but at least, when that time comes, I will not have to worry any more about the bad publicity generated by the sinking of the *Titanic* and all who sailed in her.

Lost in the Echo

LOST IN THE ECHO: LET me explain. I am an experienced potholer and had come to explore this little-known set of caves in Southern France. It is called the echo because it is haunted by strange sounds and echoes. Finding myself in a large cavern with six tunnels leading away, I was uncertain of the way to go.

"Help! I'm lost!" I shouted. "Lost!" came back the echo.

"Anybody there?" The echo came again, "there ..." and suddenly, standing a few feet in front of me, was another caver. She was tall and graceful with long curled tresses of red hair hanging over a diaphanous green dress, an unusual attire for a caver.

"I am lost," I said.

"Lost!" she echoed.

"Can you help me?"

"Me!" she echoed, pointing to herself with her echo.

Suddenly I realized that this apparition must be Echo, the nymph who helped Zeus to deceive his wife Hera by distracting her with chatter. Echo was punished by being deprived of the power to say anything except the last syllable of whatever she heard.

"Who are you?"

"You!" she pointed at me.

It was frustrating. I tried to think of words which would hopefully lead me to the cave's entrance.

"These caves, can I get out?"

"Out!" she pointed to one of the six exits.

"Will you come?" I said.

"Come!" the echo was most welcome this time as she led me along the tunnel pointed out. I followed at a respectful distance wishing that I had a more powerful torch to illuminate her sylph like figure. All too soon we came to the cave's entrance.

"Thank you," I said.

"You," she replied, "are the hundredth person I have helped from this cave and now the curse of the Gods has been lifted. I can now talk as normal."

"You have a lovely voice. We can chatter all day if you wish," I enthused.

"I must go now," she said.

"Can I give you a big hug goodbye?"

"No, I'm sorry but I am not allowed physical contact with a mortal being, but I will visit you in your dreams." With this she disappeared.

"Give my regards to Zeus!" I shouted as I walked into the bright sunlight. A small town nestled far below in the valley and the enchanting music of children playing in the distance came gently on the breeze. It had been a momentous day. I had been lost in the echo, found by Echo and now promised Echo in my dreams. I sat down at the cave's entrance to have forty winks before descending to the town far below.

Return to the Echo

I DECIDED TO RETURN TO the Echo cave in Southern France exactly a year after my first visit, when I had lost my way in the cave and was rescued by the nymph 'Echo.' She had regained her ability to speak after rescuing the one hundredth potholer from the labyrinth. The person whom she had rescued was me, and I had fallen for her glorious looks and beautiful voice and hoped to see her again as my valentine. She had promised to visit me in my dreams but had not, as yet, appeared.

The Echo cave was the same with its labyrinth of tunnels and I carefully marked my trail so that I would be able to find my way out if necessary. Reaching the central cavern with its six tunnels leading off, I shouted her name, and listened to the multiplicity of echoes which were returned.

The Goddess Echo appeared before me but, oh my God, she had changed. Her flaming red, waist long hair had been cropped short and, instead of wearing a shimmering green dress of silk, she was dressed in an old boiler suit and was carrying three clipboards in her arms.

"Hush," her voice had deepened and coarsened. "You will wake Morpheus, the God of sleep with that noise and he will have a dreadful hangover and demand more poppies than are good for him."

"I'm sorry." I replied, then "You've changed."

"Yes, I have changed, but I remember you. I was liberated from the echo curse when I rescued you from the cave a year ago. However, since then, Zeus my boss has put me in charge of the fight against global warming and has asked me to change my name to Eco. I am also undergoing gender reassignment and taking celestial hormone therapy in the land of the gods.

"Do you like the change?" she asked.

She must have read my thoughts because she suddenly changed the subject and told me that she had visited me several times in my dreams.

"I don't remember the visits."

"I came at three o'clock in the morning, the darkest and quietest time of the night."

"My alarm clock is set for eight o'clock," I replied. "It would have been better if you could have come fifteen minutes before that time. I always remember dreams round about then." We were both silent for a moment, then I said. "I brought my iPhone with me today. I thought I might be able to take a selfie with you but I'm not so sure I want to do that now."

Echo, or Eco as she was now called, looked nonplussed. She obviously wanted to placate me. "I'll tell you what. I will summon the goddess of love, Aphrodite, and we can all have a photo together." Aphrodite duly appeared: she smelt strongly of seaweed, having been formed from the foam of the sea, and, though she had a gorgeous figure, she lacked a pair of arms.

"I lost them from a bad case of meningeal sepsis," she said reading my thoughts. "But it does not prevent me from doing my work for the environment and women's rights. At present... " She paused importantly. "I am trying to persuade the museum curator at the Louvre in Paris to remove my statue as it is demeaning to my sex. I am also writing a book on romantic love titled *Fifty Shades of Consent*. All this while clearing the oceans of plastic waste thrown down by mortals like yourself."

"It would not be a case of all hands on deck to accomplish this task," I thought to myself looking at her figure. "No wonder the plastic in the seven seas is worsening by the day."

"No need to be flippant," said Aphrodite in her most schoolmarm voice. "You must go now."

"Have you any messages for Zeus?" Eco tried to cool the situation. "Last time we met, you told me to give him your regards."

"You can tell him to go easy on the #MeToo's," I said grumpily. At this, I was frogmarched to the entrance of the cave by the two Goddesses and flung outside despite them saying they could not have contact with mortal beings. I sat down on a large stone as they disappeared.

The soothing sounds of the village far below me gradually seeped into my consciousness: the faint hum of traffic, the occasional shouts of workers in the fields and the immortal music of children at play in the distance. This was the real world and I resolved to seek my valentine there, despite its faults. I also made a mental note to set my alarm for twenty past three in the morning instead of eight o'clock, in the hope that Echo would visit me as Echo and not as Eco.

Rearranging the Deckchairs

As president of the Company, I had the important task of interviewing candidates for the job of rearranging deckchairs on the ocean liner the *Titanic*. I was impressed by the wide range of talent applying for the position and one of the applicants, a certain Mr Nero and an emperor by trade, showed great promise. He was an accomplished violinist and would be an asset to the ship's orchestra in his spare time. He impressed the committee by his mettle in rallying his countrymen by playing his fiddle to them while the barbarians were at the gates of Rome.

"Would you have time to carry out the job as well as fulfil your important position in Rome?" I asked him.

"Rome was not burnt down in a day," he quoted in answer and he assured us that he would not suddenly dash back to Rome to take part in the *Decline and Fall of the Roman Empire*.

Two candidates were unsuitable: a Mr Todd, an obscure barber from Sweden had a great deal of experience with reclining chairs but worried the committee by gesticulating with his cut-throat razor while answering questions. His obsession with pies and his assertion that he could cut the cost of the liner's meat bill were also vaguely unsettling.

Mr Neptune was even more unsuitable. With long straggly hair and a strong smell of seaweed, he came to the interview holding a large trident. His main claim to the job was that he could continue even if the *Titanic* sank. Also, in the middle of the interview, he completely spoilt his chance of the job when he used his trident to spear a large watermelon from a bowl of fruit in the middle of the table and began eating it in a most disgusting manner.

In the end, the committee decided to give the post to a certain Mr Jobsworth from the Edinburgh Traffic Department.

"I will draw yellow lines on the deck and put a parking meter by each deckchair." He told us enthusiastically. "I will also ticket those who oversleep their time on the chairs and issue fines to passengers who plonk themselves down on the deck between deckchairs". He was a real go-getter from the Blue Meanies and would earn extra money for the company.

Unfortunately, the *Titanic* sank some days after this interview and Mr Jobsworth was unable to take up his post. We offered him a position on the Belfast jetty, but he declined as he wanted to go to sea. He told me that he had taken a job as a midshipman on an old sailing ship called the *Bounty*. What happened to him after that? Well, I guess I'll never know.

A Difficult Journey on Deep Sussex Rail

I HAD BOUGHT MY TICKET well in advance, anticipating some minor problems on the way, but nothing prepared me for the difficulties encountered on this journey on Deep Sussex Rail. The problems started when I tried to get through the station barrier: my ticket was refused acceptance at the barrier and a railway official clawed his way across a seething mob to see what was up.

He looked at me suspiciously. "This is yesterday's train," he announced importantly. "Your ticket is for today's train which isn't due here until tomorrow."

"You can't use this ticket," he added.

"Can I not get a ticket for yesterday's train en route?" I asked hopefully.

"Can't help that," replied Jobsworth but I was saved by the pressure of the crowd behind me which propelled me through the barrier, and I sped through the crowded platform to its furthest point.

"The train arriving at platform four," shouted Bouncer the announcer, "is the eight forty-five to Deep Sussex Terminus in London. We apologise for the twenty-four-hour delay which was caused by unforeseen variations of current in the overhead wires."

"Wrong kind of electrons," I thought as I was pushed into a carriage by the mass of people behind me. I ended up crushed against a buxom young woman who spat poison through an icy smile.

The train jerked to a start, rattled forward for a few miles but gradually came to a wheezing halt at the approach to the South Downs. "This is where we jettison some of our cargo," said a man standing next to me. "Come back a bit from the door."

The guard and the catering manager, together with several passengers, were manhandling the drinks trolley towards the door where I stood and the guard opened the carriage door.

"They're not going to push the trolley out?" I said aghast.

"They are and it makes good sense," said my fellow passenger. "This will lighten our load to get us moving and it's much cheaper to dispense with the trolley than send a helicopter to take off passengers. Also, a trolley service is impossible when the train is so crowded," he added. "It's rotten coffee at any rate."

There was a series of crashes as the trolley rolled down the embankment and, sure enough, the train started to move with a wheeze and a groan. A disembodied voice came after us from the embankment, "Would you like one or two teaspoons of sugar in your coffee, sir?"

Good taste precludes me from telling about other incidents on the journey but, after a scrum worthy of the Six Nations tournament at the terminus, I decided to walk across London to Far Northern Terinus for my onward journey to Glasgow.

A Guided Tour of the Deep Sussex Railway Museum

"ATTENTION PLEASE! TIME FOR THE next tour." An authoritative voice rang out above the general level of conversation in a group of people waiting to be shown round the railway museum at Deep Sussex Terminus. "Time gentlemen please: All your glasses!" The tour guide was a former barman who had not shaken off former habits of speech and the waiting group gradually became silent in expectation. "I'm here to show you round this splendid museum but before we go, I would like to direct your attention to this large clock on the wall here. This is a forty-eight-hour clock and was specially made for us because our trains were often more than twenty-four hours late. It made forward planning easier."

"The little office on the right is the old ticket office. If you look carefully at some of the old tickets, you may notice that the following day is stamped over the date of issue. This is also due to the trains being a day late. There was some confusion at first, but passengers soon became used to our methods. Now we will enter the Grand Foyer."

The guide led the group through to a large hall where an ancient tank engine was coupled to a more modern carriage. "This is our prize exhibit," the guide intoned proudly. "It was called *Thomas the Tank Engine* but was known locally as *The Doubting Thomas* since it was never certain whether it would make it over the South Downs. The carriage at the back is more modern and, on the step to greet you is our museum beauty, Miss Railcar. She used to be given the grand title, Miss Carriage but that had to change.

"Why was that?" said a voice from the crowd.

"Well ... er ... she became pregnant. Now, let's go inside." Miss Railcar gave the visitors a radiant smile as the group entered the carriage and the guide told them that although the seating capacity was fifty-six, there had been one hundred and twenty-three travellers crammed in on one journey near Deep Sussex Croydon junction at one point.

"Some crush," another voice from the crowd. "Is that why the handrails are bent, and the luggage rack broken?"

"Just so," explained the tour guide. "We had to put up a notice saying, '*Only Children and Adults Weighing Less Than Ten Stone Allowed to Lie Along the Luggage Racks*.' Now, at the end of the carriage here, we have one of our drinks trolleys which was rescued from the railway embankment a few years ago. Many of these had to be pushed off the train, on the steep gradient up the South Downs to allow the train to get over the top of the hill."

"What a waste of gin and tonic." A small wiry man was examining the battered trolley closely.

"It was cheaper doing this than evacuating the passengers or sending a relief engine," said the guide. "And sir," he said sharply, "Do not sample the drinks. The trolley was pulled from a puddle of water and diesel at the foot of the embankment."

The visitors were hustled out of the carriage into a small side room where a solitary toilet sat in the centre of the room surrounded by railings. "This is one of our notorious toilets," explained the guide. "The lid was, unfortunately, precariously balanced and would crash down if the train went over a bump. Cost us a lot of money for injuries, it did. Health and Safety made us enclose it with a fence after a visitor cheekily tried to use it in the museum when no-one was watching. Poor chap, should have been a foot taller … Sir!" he shouted, "Will you stop poking your finger through the railings."

The guided tour ended shortly after that. Everyone clapped as the guide directed them to the museum shop, "Many happy memories to buy," he told them. "And our speciality line is a miniature drinks trolley you can push around the kitchen table top. Have a good day."

Harvest Time on Deep Sussex Rail

I BOARDED DEEP SUSSEX RAIL feeling well pleased with myself. Ryanair had given me a free flight as I had carried all my luggage in special pockets made for my jacket and I had required none of their overpriced extras. Even an apology for their services, which probably would have cost twenty pounds, had been avoided. The train was very crowded, and I had to avoid swinging my coat with its heavy pockets. Things go amiss though: with the train slowing down for Deep Clapham junction and masses of desperate commuters thronging past me, an angry voice from a seat almost below me, caught my attention.

"You sir!" exclaimed a country-looking gentleman angrily. "Look what you've done with your coat. You banged into my laptop with something in your pocket and made me buy one hundred concubine harvesters instead of one as I intended."

"Concubine harvesters?" I queried. "Surly you mean combine harvesters."

"No! Concubine harvesters, you clown. We country folk use them for our post-harvest celebrations. Have you never heard of 'The Ball of Kirriemuir'?"

"Oh yes," I said brightly. "That would be one of our favourite songs on the school bus in time gone by." I began to sing –

"The ball, the ball, the ball of Kirriemuir,
Four and twenty ... "

He cut me short. "Well, what are you going to do about it?"

"I'm sorry." I said. "Do you not have a fourteen-day cooling off period for cancelling the order? This is usually the case." Privately, I thought that with a hundred of these things, there would be no cooling off period within fourteen years.

The train came to a sudden halt at the station, and I knew what I was going to do about it. I made a beeline for the door before he could follow and battled against the incoming throng to get onto the platform. The last I saw of him was a red face and a fist shaking behind the window.

Raking in my coat pockets for my rail ticket, I realised that one of my wallets was missing. I must have dropped it on the floor of the train when the coat hit against the computer. The wallet contained five hundred euros but fortunately not my credit cards or other forms of identification. It was a loss which I would not be following up. He could buy two harvesters with my five hundred euros and might even get some 'Ooh La La' foreign entertainment with the depreciation of the pound against the euro. I realised, however, that I had not saved any money on this trip.

Love in a Rough Climate

SITTING ON A GRASSY VERGE at the side of the road, Dave was studying his trusty map. He looked up as a shadow fell across the map. A girl of his own age was standing there, dressed as untidily as himself and staring down at him. He recognised a fellow hitch hiker. "Hi! Where are you going?" she asked carelessly but warily.

"Just over the pass here," he indicated a point about five inches across the map. She stood back a pace. "Have something to eat," said Dave. "What's your name by the way?"

"Susan."

"I'm Dave," he replied. "Came from Paris in the last four days. Lucky to do that. France is lousy for hitch-hiking since the new car insurance laws were introduced."

"What's that?" she answered nonchalantly but nevertheless widening her narrow eyes a little.

"If you're a driver in this country and you're carrying a hitch-hiker, you can't claim insurance if involved in a crash."

She said nothing. Just munched hungrily her bread and sausage.

"How come you've just landed here?" queried Dave. "I usually meet female hitch-hikers like you only at youth hostels ... sitting wearing dark glasses ... sipping Coca-Cola and looking frightfully intellectual. Where are all your friends?"

"I lost my companions in Landslebourgh. That's over the high pass where you're going. I also lost my money in the process." She did not elaborate on this.

"That's bad. You're making for the channel?"

"Yes, but I don't know if I'll get there. I've no money."

"Have you tried the British Consulate?"

"There's no Consulate near here. They're a bit cagey. Also, too many claims by destitute travellers like myself."

No money thought Dave. She was being pretty brass necked about it. OK, but she probably was being honest about the situation since she must have been in a passing car and asked the driver to stop when she saw him sitting at the side of the road. He pondered a moment.

"Why not come along with me?" he said casually. "I have enough money for two people. You would have to live a bit rough, and you might have to sleep under the stars, but there would be enough to eat if you don't take a fourth helping as you're doing at present. We could cuddle up together in our sleeping bags to keep warm and dream about tomorrow.

"Separate sleeping bags?"

"Certainly," said Dave. "I don't want mine further damaged."

She was an attractive girl under these rather grimy clothes, and she would smell of the open air. It would be a good deal for both and he would be glad of her companionship if nothing else. "All right," she said with a short laugh. She narrowed her expressive steel grey eyes and helped herself to another round of continental sausage and bread while he resumed his study of the squiggles on his map which represented unknown and fascinating glaciers.

They were given a lift twenty or so miles up the valley and left from a small village after collecting provisions for the next two days. The way was always up along the dusty road, but the ascent was gradual. Along the river, a large patch of dark grey snow lay from the previous winter. Below this, a tributary of the Isère fell vertically from the unseen glaciers of Mont Pourri.

"Can we stop here? I'm tired," said Susan.

"Good idea." Dave was pensive. There were still enough sticks for a fire from the thinning vegetation and he built a small fire and laid out his Lilo for them both to sit on. He then produced a small pan to cook some eggs and the rest of the continental sausage.

After the supper, the light was failing rapidly, though the snow-capped peaks around Mont Blanc still glowed brilliantly in a long-gone sun. Dave unpacked his sleeping bag and placed it on his Lilo before wriggling into it. Susan stood watching with a sullen look on her face, her own sleeping bag dangling from one hand. "Come on over," called Dave, "you'll soon get cold out there."

"Just coming, if that's what you want," she gave a sudden laugh and brought the sleeping bag up beside him, giggling as if it were a huge joke. She then proceeded to push him over to try to claim half the Lilo. But it did not work out however hard they struggled to make themselves comfortable on half a Lilo. Eventually, Dave gave up and walked round to the other side of his companion. He lifted her up in her sleeping bag and placed her gently on the Lilo. He snuggled up as close as possible on the hard ground and slid his hand over her sleeping bag to feel the soft contours of her body through several layers of cloth. She suddenly gave a small cry and sat up immobile and stiff.

Dave recoiled a little and shone a small torch onto her face. It was expressionless but a teardrop, like a flashing diamond in the light of the torch, was running down her cheek. "I'm sorry," he said quietly. "I've hurt you."

She did not respond.

"I'll roll over away from you and switch off the sun to leave you in peace," he added.

He did this and, after a few minutes, was gratified to feel her snuggle up more closely into his back. He fell asleep with the delicious memory of lifting her lithe body onto his precious Lilo.

The Long Hard Trek

IT WAS THE DONE THING in the 1960's: university students took advantage of the long summer breaks to hitch-hike or cycle round Europe if they had not spent all their grant money on drinking beer and singing student university songs while dancing on top of the student university bar. Desmond and his friend Olivia had taken advantage of the long hot summer of 1965 to go on a cycling trip in the best regions of France. They had travelled through the Alps from Nice, over the highest pass in Europe at 9,085 feet and were now in northern France heading for the Vosges, a chain of rounded, conifer covered hills parallel to the hills of the Black Forest in Germany.

"A sair fecht," grumbled Desmond. The youth hostels, unlike those in Britain, were often over one hundred miles apart and the pair had to sleep in the open from time to time, though the nights, as well as the days, were always very warm.

"Shouldn't be too bad today," said Susan. "This next hostel is only sixty miles from the last and the road's fairly level here." The two of them cycled briskly along the quiet French road, chattering lazily from time to time and admiring the large fields of sweetcorn plants, guarded by their rustic owners, who occasionally sported a shotgun over their shoulder. "Nice people," said Susan.

Beyond the small town of Lautenbach, the countryside gradually changed. The hills became more densely forested, and the going was steadily uphill. A few miles further on, the intrepid pair came to a small village where the youth hostel was marked on the map. They stopped to ask, in broken French, where the hostel was situated and were pointed to a hill on the left and a rough track leading into the forest.

"I hope it's not too far," said Susan. "It's been a long day and I'm looking forward to a good sleep." Hopes were gradually dashed, however, as the track wound on and on with the sun slowly sinking below the top of the ridge in a blaze of glory. Desmond estimated them to have climbed about two thousand feet above the valley far below when a small broken-down sign indicated the way to the hostel: a small path leading further up the hill to the left.

"It's certainly a long trek, especially with a heavy cycle to push," Susan mused as she had to lift it over a small fallen log but neither she, nor her companion, wanted to camp out in the forest as the air was becoming chilly though the large red ants were still active and busy everywhere on the forest floor. These ants were twice the size of the large red ants in Britain, but they did not seem to bite or sting, though they looked very vicious. Oilskin capes seemed to repel these creatures, though a few nights ago, a mass of them had gathered to finish off an uneaten sandwich left at the edge of one of the oilskin capes.

The path climbed steadily to the crest of the hill and a silvery moon on the right came out to cast a mystic light in the forest. Susan shivered, "Do you think there's any wolves around?" Her companion grunted, "Wolves are extremely unlikely to attack humans, especially in summer when small prey is plentiful. And there are no werewolves around either. They only come out when the moon is full." Both then trudged on in silence.

"It was almost ten o'clock when they reached the summit of the hill where a large, ramshackle building showed a guiding light in one of its windows. Susan shone a torch on the notice outside. "Twelve hundred metres, that's about four thousand feet. We're up the same height as the summit of Ben Nevis." Susan said, "Come on the last hundred yards."

The building looked spooky in the moonlight. The way up had been a long hard trek. Desmond pulled the large, ornate brass handle on the door. There was a long pause. He pulled again and ... the handle came away in his grasp.

Dilemma in a Lift

IT WAS GOING TO BE an exciting evening. The Exotic Toys and Dress Corporation were holding their annual fancy dress party on the thirteenth floor of their office headquarters. "I'm so looking forward to this evening," said Alice to her companion, the Mad Hatter, as they joined the droves of eager workers in fancy dress homing their way into the emporium on the ground floor of the building. "Drinks fortified with fairy dew!" called Lily the Pink as people entered. "And freely available, I see." The Mad Hatter doffed his hat as he passed into the babble of voices filling the emporium.

The lifts were working overtime and lift number three had just filled up with a dozen people. The doors were closing. "Sorry, can I squeeze in?" A man dressed as the Loch Ness Monster just managed to push his way in. The doors closed. Unfortunately, his tail was caught by the inner doors and the lift suddenly ground to a halt midway between the fifth and sixth floors. There was a grinding noise, followed by a shower of sparks, then silence.

A babble of confused voices arose.

"What on earth's happened?"

"Is it a power cut?"

"Are we going to crash down?"

"Something must have disturbed the electricals," said Bob the Builder. "But there are always failsafe mechanisms to stop the lift from freefalling." However voices became louder and more anxious, though the Loch Ness Monster said nothing, but shrank back against the lift door to conceal his long sad tail.

"It's no use blaming one another or the lift." A senior accountant dressed as Einstein took charge of the conversation. "I suggest we tell jokes in turn to lighten the atmosphere while we wait for rescue. I can start and this is a real cracker." Everyone stopped talking and listened to what he had to say. "What do men do standing up, women do sitting down and dogs do on three legs?"

Everyone stared at the floor wondering what to say.

"Why, they shake hands," said Einstein triumphantly, pleased at his own cleverness.

A nervous titter went round the occupants of the lift as they digested this joke. All was quiet for a few seconds. "What a stupid joke." Jack the Giant Killer broke the silence after spitting out the five beans he had obtained in exchange for his mother's cow. "You'd be better off telling us how thirteen people can get out of this lift if you think you're Einstein." Jack was unimpressed.

"Einstein was a physicist, not a hydraulic engineer." The accountant gave Jack a patronising smile. "But he would have had more chance of thinking of a way to get us out than you would of growing a beanstalk to the next floor, especially since these horrible beans have been in your mouth."

A while passed and the chatter became more despondent as there was no announcement from the intercom in the lift. No one had yet noticed the Loch Ness Monster stuck fast to the door by his tail and meanwhile Snow White was becoming more and more agitated. "I need to go to the loo," she announced at last in a loud voice. Silence followed. This prolonged pause was broken by Red Riding Hood who spoke up. She was the most sympathetic. "You can give me that large holdall," she said, turning to the Woodsman, her husband. "I know it's waterproof and has rigid sides. Everyone can turn the other way and I will hold my red cloak in front of Snow White while she goes."

Mother Earth, who had a huge globe of the world encircling her middle, was less sympathetic. "And don't fall asleep on the pot for a hundred years: I need to go next," she said cattily.

"It was the Sleeping Beauty who fell asleep for one hundred years," snapped Snow White. She added. "If you could turn your ridiculous globe round a bit, you'd have the whole of the Pacific Ocean to piss into." Snow White was no snowflake.

"Now, now," exclaimed Red Riding Hood, "no need for all this." She then fixed a steely eye on the Big Bad Wolf telling him to go right to the back of the pack. "You can give me that Ventolin inhaler of yours as well. I don't want you huffing and puffing while I protect Snow White's modesty with my cloak."

"You're getting your fairy tales mixed up," the Big Bad Wolf muttered darkly. "Just as well I did not come dressed as Taurus the bull." Everyone turned the other way except the Loch Ness Monster who could not turn, though he did produce a glossy leaflet of the Loch Ness visitor centre, which he held over his eyes while Snow White did her turn into the holdall. Much alcohol had been consumed and more people came forward for their turn. A few mishaps occurred: a small portion of Mother Earth's globe, showing the British Isles, emerged from behind the red cloak and Mother Earth was furious when someone shouted, "Brexit at last." A young woman, dressed as Rapunzel in the fairy tale, refused the offer of the cloak, saying she would let down her hair. Unfortunately, the long tresses worn on her hair caught on the handle of the holdall causing them to slip off, revealing a well-rounded bottom. "A bad hair day," she lamented mournfully.

Modesty prevailed however and soon the holdall was brimming with a shimmering amber sea, wonderful to behold. The only person not to contribute was the Loch Ness Monster, who was not able to move to the other side of the lift.

"I don't think it would be appropriate to perform an '*Arc de triomphe*' across a crowded floor." The monster was adamant. "I can wait."

"Serves you right," hissed a small wiry man dressed as a royal python. "I think you meant all this trouble."

"Rubbish," retorted Nessie. "The serpent speaks with a forked tongue."

In reply, the python stuck out a lurid green forked tongue at the Loch Ness Monster from under his collar but skipped out of reach as Nessie was much bigger than him. "I should drag you to the bottom of Loch Ness," said Nessie darkly.

The situation was saved by an announcement from the intercom. "The fault has been rectified and you should be able to get out very soon." Everyone cheered as the lift gave a sudden lurch upward. The Loch Ness Monster lurched forward, freed from the door, and slipped on the five magic beans which Jack the Giant Killer had discarded. His foot went down on the side of the holdall and a rippling amber liquid spread rapidly over the floor of the lift. There was much splashing about as everyone tried to avoid the advancing tide. It was not a night for happy feet.

"Take off your shoes," ordered Einstein as the sorry occupants exited the lift where they were greeted by Goody Two Shoes and Cinderella. "How novel," exclaimed Goody, "a number in fancy dress pretending to be penguins; or is it a troop of penguins in fancy dress?"

"Never mind her." Cinderella was more sympathetic. "You've

been through a lot. Good company is needed. Come along and p-p-p-pick up a Prosecco!"

Everyone followed Cinderella except the Loch Ness Monster, who made a quick dash to the nearest toilet, hoping his tail would not get caught again.

Dicing with Death

(Norman *is at home, seated at a small coffee table with a glass of red wine. A chessboard is on the table, ready for a game.* Norman *dials on his iPhone*)

NORMAN. Hello, is that Deep Sussex Rail Pizza Express? I'd like to order a pizza with chillies. Also, one of your death by chocolate emperor muffins for a sweet. Make it snappy. I'm dying of hunger. Thank you ... see you in fifteen minutes.

(*Enter a figure wearing a black hood and carrying a scythe in his right hand, and a clipboard in his left*)

NORMAN. Who the hell are you?

FIGURE. I am the grim reaper, or Death. You said you were dying and I have come for your soul.

NORMAN. You've got the wrong person bud. I feel perfectly well and I was just ordering a pizza when you rudely interrupted me.

DEATH. Nevertheless, you have been assigned a place in the hereafter (*consults his clipboard*) You may confirm it if you wish. The phone number for Heaven is 007 777.

(Norman *dials and listens for a few seconds on his iPhone. He then turns back to death*)

NORMAN. The good Lord says he has no place for me. He's looking for someone for the Hallelujah choir, someone who can sing or play an instrument. I can do neither.

DEATH. You must phone Hell then. The number is 007 666.

(Norman *dials again and listens for a few seconds. He then turns back to face Death again.*)

NORMAN. That's odd. Satan does say he has a place for me. I'm a qualified engineer and he needs someone to service his speedboat. I did not know the devil had a speedboat.

DEATH. That's one of his punishments in Hell. The Devil cruises around the evil smelling pits and sends waves over the heads of lost souls who are standing neck deep in sewage. Now, are you coming with me?

NORMAN. I'm not ready to die. What about a game of chess to decide the issue? You know like in the film *The Seventh Seal*, a Swedish production that came out a few years ago. If you win, you can have my soul. If I win you must leave me alone.

DEATH. Okay, we will play while you wait for that muffin you ordered.

(*They start to play. After several moves,* Norman *makes a quick swoop and jubilantly confronts* Death)

NORMAN. That's fool's mate! I've won and now you must leave me.

DEATH. That's odd. I've never lost a game before this.

NORMAN. Where Death is thy sting-a-ling, where grave thy victoree?

(Death *backs away two paces.* Norman *looks more assertive*)

NORMAN. Be gone Death. You have plenty of material for your scythe elsewhere.

(Death *walks away but pauses after a few paces and turns*)

DEATH. I'll be back!

NORMAN. Beat it Arnie and shut the door on the way out. I don't want to catch my death of cold after all this.

(*Exit* Death. Norman *takes out his iPhone again and dials*)

NORMAN. Hello ... Pizza Express? ... Can I change my order? A king size pizza without chillies and cancel the death by chocolate muffin. Can you also deliver a large bottle of red wine? Casillero del Diablo will be just fine ... Thank you.

(Norman *picks up his glass and raises it in a toast*)

NORMAN. Here's to my computer assisted chess board linked to *Deep Blue*.

Hunting the Haggis

THIS ARTICLE IS ON THE noble sport of haggis hunting and, before anything else, I would like to dispel the belief that the haggis lives in the nineteenth hole of the golf course. This myth was probably originated by the drinks trade and has been perpetuated by generations of schoolboys, usually as crude jokes. Another myth is that the haggis has one leg longer than the other, an evolutionary device that allows it to outpace predators by running around the sides of steep slopes. This of course is nonsense: the slight advantage of such asymmetry on say, the steep slopes of a Scottish ben, would be greatly outweighed by the disadvantages of flat ground as occurs on Rannoch moor.

The habitat of the haggis is, however, the wilds of Scotland and a concentration of the creatures occurs in the mountains and glens near Balmoral castle where the presence of security personnel has, presumably, discouraged the presence of hunters. Prince Charles has written a short book about these fascinating creatures a number of years ago. Most people think that hunting the haggis is much the same as grouse shooting since the seasons are almost the same. There are however a number of important differences. Grouse shooting involves a line of beaters, usually students on their summer vacation, lining up at roughly one-hundred-yard intervals and driving the birds towards a set of butts where the guns are fired as the grouse pass overhead. The haggis, however, is a cunning and highly intelligent creature with advanced mathematical skills and would double back at fifty yards from the nearest beater who would be making too much noise to notice. Another important reason is that shooting has to be at ground level and health and safety would frown on students returning to their university studies full of lead shot. The use of dogs is also out of the question: the haggis can emit the sound of the bagpipes very loudly but at an ultrasonic frequency inaudible to the human ear. Dogs however freeze in terror and are incapacitated.

Thus, sportsmen hunting the haggis have to advance in line over the moors and this brings us to the other pitfalls of the sport. Haggises can also throw their voices, likened to the wail of the bagpipes, some considerable distance and many a hunter has shot himself in the foot or somewhere more painful when this ventriloquist device has been used by the hunted. Another problem related to this voice throwing technique is the luring of the hunter into a dangerous peat bog on a misty highland morning when the sportsmen cannot see each other and the ghostly strains of 'The Bonnie Wells o' Wearie' are often said to be heard when a haggis hunter disappears without trace on the moors. The haggis is also fiercely nationalistic. English sportsmen have a far higher chance of suffering this fate than Scots and most hunt organisers have taken to warn their charges to refrain from shouting to each other in Oxford accents if a mist descends on the hunt. Another recent defence by the haggis has been observed: some can change the colour of their skin to a pattern of stars and stripes, and this puts off American hunters who baulk at shooting at their own flag. Fortunately, the haggis has not yet been able to disguise itself as a saltire because it cannot reproduce the large areas of white colour required.

The haggis does not have everything its own way, however. They are very fond of Tunnocks tea cakes and are dopey and prone to capture while eating one of these tasty treats. Most hunters carry a supply of Tunnocks to use at opportune moments and recently, lead pellets tipped with teacake concentrate have become available to incapacitate the creatures more easily. Some regard this as unsporting though it is necessary as the haggis rapidly evolves its defences.

In summary then, hunting the haggis is a noble sport but only for the resourceful, intelligent and skilled marksman who has plenty of money. If an individual has more than plenty of money, the other conditions can be waived. An alternative for the average individual is to attend a Burns supper or invest in Haggopoly, a board game rather like Monopoly where players chase and shoot the haggis round the board with all the excitement and pitfalls of the hunt. Further details may be had at the website huntingthehaggis@scot. uk Good luck and happy hunting.

The Spot On Breakfast Show
Discusses Climate Change

A YOUNG WOMAN, SEATED ON a couch, peers at the television camera through an atmosphere of thick gushiness in the television studio. "Good morning all you lovely persons. My name is Tallulah and I am hosting the *Spot On Breakfast Show*. Today is all about climate change and I have three experts with me in the studio to give their views on global warming, which is now an emergency." The TV camera pans to three individuals seated opposite Tallulah and eager to start proceedings.

Tallulah preens herself in front of the camera. "On the right I have Al Hardman who owns a large ranch in California. In the middle, Professor Clarence Toohey from the Faculty of Woke at Deep Sussex Rail University and on the left Noel Wright, a journalist from Lancashire who writes for the *Weekly Review*. We had arranged to have a young activist from Sweden, but her sailing boat was becalmed midway when one of the sailors took a pot shot at an oversized seagull, which was harassing the crew and stealing their ice creams. She is still stuck with a load of ancient mariners. I'll start with you Al. You have come in your private jet. Very commendable considering Covid, but how do you square your carbon footprint with climate change."

"Howdy folk. I'm Al and president of the Entitled Elite Society Against Global Warming. I have offset my carbon footprint by killing off five hundred head of cattle and planting five thousand trees in their place."

"Are they deciduous trees or conifers?"

"I'm not sure. Could only buy very small trees so I bought nice large plastic ones instead. These will last much longer and probably do the same job."

"Very commendable. I'm sure you've given our audience much to think about." Tallulah now turns to the second guest. "Now it's your turn Professor Toohey. I note that you have a lot of experience in climate change. Can you give our audience more details?"

"Yes, I am Professor of Gender Studies at the University, but this sometimes includes work on the effects of transphobia on global warming. I discuss the climate emergency with colleagues ... and I also read the Guardian."

"Do you think this entitles you to be an expert on climate?"

"Yes, because I'm always right and everyone else is wrong. I'm also a member of Extinction Rebellion and support Insulate Britain."

"And I suppose your house is well insulated?"

"No, but it does not matter because thousands of other houses, throughout the area, have not been insulated. Also, I have a fine Georgian mansion which would be spoiled by insulation and double glazing."

"That's a very common-sense point of view," says Tallulah soothingly. "You're obviously doing a great deal of work for the prevention of climate change. I'll now turn to our third guest for his qualifications and his views on the climate emergency."

"I have no qualifications," answers Noel. "And I am not an expert. I think that the only reason that I was invited here to speak is that your show is now able to stir the witches cauldron of misinformation to further your own fashionable points of view."

"So, you're a climate change denier?"

"Not so, I do believe in global warming and that it is manmade. However, I also believe that the governments are doing as much as possible to prevent warming without creating a situation where future generations are huddled over candles to keep warm when the sun does not shine, and the wind does not blow."

"A lot of people would find your views abhorrent. What do you say to that?"

"… I have a good supply of candles."

"And what do you think of the activists in Extinction Rebellion and Insulate Britain?"

"I admire them for their courage and tenacity, especially the older more mature individuals, but I also think some of their activities are counterproductive. Blocking the slip roads to motorways is stupid and dangerous. These activists have a right to protest but should glue themselves to the grass verges of the slip roads instead of the tarmac where they would be closer to nature. They'd also be more identifiable to the police with their turfs of grass growing from their nether regions."

"Anything else to say?"

"Yes, unlike Professor Toohey, I am willing to admit I could be wrong until proven right if you can see what I mean."

"I do see what you mean but I don't agree with your sentiments." Tallulah looks at the clock. "My time's up. My thanks to my three guests and the audience for the excellent and informed discussion on climate change though I would say, if I were not completely unbiased, that I find Noel's contribution disappointing. Good night and stay safe."

The guests file out of the studio and the cameras fade out.

Songwriters' Symposium 2119

THE HALL WAS VIBRANT. THERE was no buzzing of human voices since the participants were all robots or androids at this annual convention of songwriters 2119. A hush fell over the audience as the Grand Grinder, as he was called, entered from the back of the stage.

"Fellow androids and robots," he announced, "tonight we celebrate the works of this year's songwriters and also the twenty-fifth anniversary of the mechanisation of the human race." The clinks and whirrs of the audience stopped for a moment, then they all burst into their signature anthem *Technik Über Alles*.

"We now come to the prizes for the song of the year," the Grand Grinder announced. "The third prize goes to Heavy Metal Loaf for his stirring lyric *The Factories Are Alive With The Sound Of Music*. This has nuts and bolts chiming away in the background and has great rhythm with its combination of tap and screw."

"The second prize has been won by Tin Pan Sally with her song *I Want a Robot Man to Hold Me Tight*. Based on a popular song from the 1960's, this lyric has great rhythm and melody and is destined to become a classic. The prize is a golden nut and bolt filled with the best penetrating oil. Step up Sally and be careful not to spill the contents." Tin Pan sallied up to the stage and skipped back down again with her prize.

"But there is no doubt as to the quality of the song which has won the first prize." The Grand Grinder glowed with electronic enthusiasm. "This song was written by Marvin, despite his bipolar condition and shows great sensitivity and insight. Called *The Ballad of TEC 18/1*, it's a highly emotional lyric about the 2107 plague caused by the infectious rust virus and the robot who nurses his partner through her fatal illness. The last verse is particularly poignant as TEC 18/1 finally rusts away. Marvin, come up and receive your well-deserved prize."

Marvin, who was depressed, climbed slowly up to the stage but suddenly slipped on a patch of penetrating oil spilt by Sally. He fell heavily down the steps to the horror of the audience but was helped to his feet by members of the audience who collected the nuts, bolts and diodes shed during his fall. Fortunately, he was still able to function well enough to collect his prize.

The Grand Grinder saved the day as he announced, "the prize for this song is a high-quality DIY kit with many spare parts, as well as the latest in tarnish resistant titanium tools and is particularly appropriate in the circumstances."

The audience clapped and again sang their anthem *Technik Über Alles*.

Suitable Candidate

I WAS VERY PLEASED TO be made chairman of the committee to interview candidates for the post of 'Director of the Regional Blood Transfusion Service'. It was an important post for a large area of the country. All the candidates were well informed and enthusiastic so it would be a difficult decision.

The third candidate, in particular, impressed me. He was stately in bearing and courteous, though his attire for the interview was slightly unusual: a long black cape over his smart suit. He explained this was because he was a Count as well as a doctor and he suffered from photophobia. He could therefore cover his eyes in bright sunlight. There was a smile and a good morning for everyone as he entered and sat down for the interview.

I said, "You seem very enthusiastic, Doctor Dracula. Can you tell me how you would improve the service if offered this post?" He leaned forward with a wolfish smile and said, "I'm sure I could improve your night service at the local hospital after a little flapping around, and, as far as the Regional Transfusion Service is concerned, I have had a lot of experience in persuading people to donate blood. I will be able to guarantee a plentiful supply of fresh blood, particularly in the winter months when donors are scarce." He told the committee that he had a three-hundred-year history of managing the transfusion services in his native Transylvania and would like to share his experience and expertise with the professionals in the United Kingdom.

After the interviews, we discussed the candidates. I was in favour of Doctor Dracula but, in the end, the committee decided against him on the grounds that he lacked a detailed knowledge of blood component therapy. The Health and Safety member also thought that Doctor Dracula's long cape might be caught in the revolving doors at the front of the building, or worse, in the doors of the blood fridges, causing a rise in temperature and spoilage of the pints for transfusion.

The committee decided instead to employ the fifth candidate who had a detailed knowledge of transplant techniques which the centre was developing with the hospitals transplant unit. His name was Doctor Frankenstein, and everyone was satisfied with this appointment.

After the interviews, I went outside to a lovely sunny afternoon where I noticed that a small patch of cloth, obviously from Doctor Dracula's cape, had been caught on the revolving door. Just beyond this, someone had left a small pile of ashes in the way, and I asked the groundsman to sweep this up before the Health and Safety expert made this a ten-man job.

The Sprout Police

THERE WAS A KNOCK AT my front door at the beginning of January. I opened the door to see two officers in a uniform I had not seen before: high vis jackets with a decoration of a large cabbage on the front. They held what looked like submachine guns at the ready.

"You know what it's about," said the more aggressive of the pair. "We're the Sprout Police."

I tried to think. "You mean I have been using a teapot with two spouts? What's wrong with that?"

"No, the **Sprout** Police!" the officer replied producing his identity card. "I'm Inspector Sproutworth and this is my assistant Sergeant Sproutright, appropriate names for our important functions, eh?"

"Yes, very, but it's a good job you're not sanitary inspectors."

"The hustles from Brussels," his companion joined in the conversation. "Data collected from your iPhone by the Council show that you took a picture of your Christmas dinner with eight brussel sprouts on one of your plates. The Council policy is that you can only have six at any one meal to prevent bad breath and other smells."

Taken aback, I explained that my children did not like sprouts and I thought I could have their allocation.

"No, that's not correct. It does not get rid of the problem of bad odours. Now, we will have to inspect your food bin."

"Can you leave your machine guns outside?" I said nervously.

"These are spray guns," said Sproutworth pointing his weapon at me. "They contain British Anti-brusselyte, an antidote to Brussel sprouts. It's similar to BAL, used to treat mustard gas poisoning." The pair raked through my food bin with eager fingers for further evidence. "What's this?" said Sproutworth, uncovering a dark green leaf.

"That's a piece of holly which fell into the bin by mistake."

"We will have to find out." He grabbed the leaf and let out a howl of anguish as the holly leaf emerged stuck fast to the end of his finger. *What a prick* I thought.

The pair decided to finish off the proceedings. "We will have to issue you with a warning. We use an e-warning instead of a written warning nowadays. It's easier."

"There's also the advantage of spellcheck," I said.

Afterwards, depressed, I watched them striding off down the road to their smart Council limousine but I cheered up when Sproutworth slid on the smooth glassy ice of the ungritted pavement and fell heavily on his back, banging his head. He would have got up more readily if the pavement had featured the large pothole full of soft snow which was present on the road nearby, but that's life. You cannot have everything your own way.

Mad as Hell

THE NIGHTMARE BEGAN AS I was sitting reading about Brexit negotiations and muttering to myself *mad as Hell*. A figure appeared: a cavernous figure wearing a black hood. "I'm Pluto, the guardian of Hell's gates. I have come to confront you about your repeated slurs on my master's territories," the figure intoned. "Satan is displeased with you for muttering 'Mad as Hell' all the time. You will come with me for an educational visit to show you we are not mad."

"I don't want to go to Hell," I replied. "You can go to Hell!"

"You will have to come," said Pluto and in a trice we were at Hell's gates, through which I was propelled without ceremony. Inside, I saw a large building with a gigantic poster of a wine bottle surrounded by flames. "This is our mildest punishment," Pluto told me. "A supermarket which sells only one product, a red wine called Casillero del Diablo. It's advertised on TV as wine from the Devil's cellar and damned souls queue everlastingly to purchase it. However, the demon on the checkout makes purchase impossible by asking them their age. We request it in decades which makes everyone under the age of twenty-five."

"It's not mad." I said. "And it certainly conserves wine stocks."

"Thank you," Pluto looked pleased. "Now come." He led me past several punishments including a lake of sewage where the Devil's speedboat showered its contents over the heads of the unlucky occupants. He also showed me the familiar mountain with souls toiling up with large boulders. "We must have punishments," proclaimed Pluto. "That's the function of Hell."

We moved on to the last punishment and in the distance, I could see souls of the damned chained to rocks with a medley of demons shooting flames at them. "This is Hell's worst fury," announced Pluto proudly.

"Why the worst?" I was curious.

"You've surely heard the saying 'Hell knows no fury like a woman scorched'. That's why," replied Pluto.

"I don't like it but it's not mad."

"I'm glad you're impressed." Pluto warmed to his presentation. "Satan has given up using fire and brimstone. High quality methane gas is used to protect the environment and the demons had been revolting against the smell of burning sulphur. They may be demons but they're only human after all."

"Very commendable. I won't say 'Mad as Hell' ever again. Can I go home now?" In a trice I was back in my own armchair. Pluto had accompanied me and asked how I felt after seeing the improvements and innovations in the underworld.

'Mad as Hell' was on the tip of my tongue but I resisted the temptation and merely said "Made Aware."

The House at the End of Spook Lane

JACK AND JILL WERE A perfect husband and wife team for their principal business in life. Although friends made jokes about them fetching pails of water, their real business was breaking and entering unoccupied premises to steal anything of value. Jack was an expert on locks and had the ability to break glass windows without a sound. Jill knew all about the value of antiques, bric-a-brac and tat.

On this moonless night, their efforts were focused on an old house which they knew had not been occupied for months. It stood dark and forbidding at the end of Spook Lane and was set in a large overgrown garden which provided excellent coverage for their nefarious activities. "It looks spooky," said Jill uncertainly. "Do you think it will be alright?"

"No werewolves wandering around the garden," answered her husband. "They only come out when the moon is full. Come on, let's get safe cracking."

Entrance to the house was easy but the solid front door hung at a slight angle and slammed behind them. The floorboards gave ghostly creaks as the pair advanced over them in the large hallway. The door of the lounge was open and a sudden movement at the far side of this room caught Jack's eye. He stiffened and held his jemmy ready to defend himself.

"It's only a mirror." Jill put her hand on his elbow to restrain him. "You almost attacked yourself just now."

"Why on earth have a mirror in an otherwise deserted room?" Jack was annoyed at having been startled.

"Perhaps the previous owners thought there was a Gorgon in the house," suggested Jill.

"A Gorgon?"

"Yes, a Gorgon." Jill gave a spooky laugh. "A Gorgon is a mythological creature which turns to stone anyone who looks at it. If you hold a mirror up to it, with your eyes shut, the Gorgon sees itself and turns itself to stone."

There was a stony silence as Jack digested this information. He sneezed as dust was disturbed and caught in his nose. "Have you noticed the smell in this room?" he said. There was indeed a sweetish, slightly fetid, odour in the room. Jill agreed. "Yes, I had noticed. It's almost exactly like that Brut aftershave you're so fond of and it's very ghostly as well as ghastly."

"Maybe the ghosts in here use aftershave," countered Jack. "Come on, let's see what's upstairs." The rooms on the second floor were empty apart from the main bedroom which had a rickety looking stepladder in one corner and some dusty paintings along one wall. The ceiling showed huge stains where water had leaked from the roof and the musty, sweet smell was overpowering; giving the room a magnificent aura of evil. All that was missing was the spooky blast of music so loved by film directors in their horror productions.

"Look!" exclaimed Jill pointing to the ceiling. "Some lovely carvings up there. Might have some value." There were indeed beautifully carved figures along the tops of the walls just below an ornate ceiling, alternate angels and demons with one angel having fallen to the floor and now smashed to pieces. "A fallen angel," muttered Jack. "Must have been unhappy with the company on each side."

"This is a handy stepladder." Jack climbed to the level of the ceiling. "I can prise off this angel here. I can hand it down it in a jiffy." Jill took it carefully and examined its delicate carvings. "It's worth a lot," she exclaimed.

"I'll take the next one down and then we can vamoose from this place. I don't like this house," said Jack as he reached for the next figure, a demon, but it suddenly and unexpectedly came away in his hand. He overbalanced and crashed down onto Jill below. The floor gave way, and both fell amongst plaster and rotten wood into the lounge below. This floor also gave way and Jack landed on what he thought was a giant rotting pumpkin in the cellar under the lounge. Jill was not so lucky. Her landing was on a small pile of builder's rubble leaving her neck at a strange angle to her body. She groaned, unable to move one leg.

A few minutes later, Jack struggled to free himself from the mess he was in. The strange, sweetish smell was now overpowering and he suddenly realised that the rotting mass was not a pumpkin, but the fruiting body of the Serpula fungus.

"There's no evil spirits in this accursed house," he groaned. "It's just bloody well riddled with ... dry rot."

A Knight in a Haunted House

BLACK THUNDERCLOUDS WERE PILING UP on the horizon behind them as Don Quixote and his assistant, Sancho, came upon an old mill in the woods. A full moon, in front of them, shone through the rotating sails of this building, creating a disturbing pattern of flashing yellow light. "We must shelter for the night in this mill," said the knight. "Do you remember that last storm when you spent three days cleaning the rust off my armour with sandpaper?"

"I don't like it." Sancho gave a slight shudder. "It looks creepy."

They knocked and the miller came to the door followed by his daughter with a come hither look in her eyes. "You may stay the night," said the miller, "But if you accost my daughter, I will grind your bones between my millstones for the day's bread."

"I am a valiant knight and a parfait gentleman according to the Spanish translation of the Canterbury Tales and your fair daughter will be quite safe," replied the knight and soon he and Sancho had settled down to a delicious meal of crusty farmhouse bread and Casillero del Diablo wine while the storm raged outside.

After supper, the miller showed the knight two small rooms at the top of the mill while Sancho attended to the horses outside the building. It was noisy in the small room allocated to Don Quixote due to the swishing of the windmill sails and the crunching of wooden cogs but eventually, the knight fell asleep.

He was woken a few hours later by a ghostly figure at the end of the bed, covered by a white sheet and sighing gently. "I am the ghost of yesterday's unwanted loaves." Then the wraith spoiled the effect by a little giggle.

"You look more like the miller's fair daughter," replied Don Quixote, the sleep in his eyes being replaced with a gleam.

"I am the miller's daughter, and I would fain make love to a valiant knight," was her reply as she quickly jumped into his bed and soon Don Quixote found her even more delicious than a crusty farmhouse loaf. She left after an hour, which both found most satisfactory, and the knight fell asleep again dreaming of fair maidens with a crusty edge to them.

He was wakened again, just before dawn, by a noise and a wraith like figure at the door. "You are a real ghost," exclaimed the knight, poking his lance through the figure and finding it difficult to extract the weapon from the wooden door. The wraith spoke. "I am the ghost of tomorrow's loaves and the dead souls who went into them. I have come to warn you. The miller has a medieval microphone fitted in this room and is, even now, preparing the millstones to make you into today's loaves so that they can be fortified with calcium. You must leave now."

Sancho was woken immediately and told to saddle the horses while Don Quixote donned his armour and had his lance ready when he crept downstairs. The burly miller was waiting where the millstones were already going round but his large cudgel was no match for the valiant knight in his suit of armour and his sharp lance. Having vanquished the miller and waved goodbye to his fair daughter, Don Quixote rode off with Sancho at his side to seek further valiant deeds.

"This is another fine mess you've got me into," he told Sancho remembering his last encounter with the ancestors of Laurel and Hardy. "I was hoping to have some more of that crusty farmhouse loaf for breakfast, and now, I shall have to seek the services of a panel beater for a large dent in my armour."

There's a 'Ye Olde Tesco Bakery' a few miles further on," said Sancho consolingly. "They sell all sorts of loaves there, everything from crusty farmhouse to Hovis seeded ... every little helps." Don Quixote grumbled for a while and ever after, he attacked a windmill with his lance if he encountered one. This is where the saying 'tilting at windmills' comes from.

The Haunted DVD ... a Halloween Story

It was the evening of the 31st October and my doorbell rang for the third time as a gaggle of witches and vampires gathered in my porch under the watchful eye of an adult in the background. I gave a pound into their tin and a Ferrero Rocher into each pair of grubby hands.

As they turned to leave, one of the little witches handed me a packet which she said had been left at the front door. I took this in, my curiosity aroused and, opening the packet, I found a shiny new DVD labelled *Nightmare on Elm Street*. I nearly dropped it when it spoke to me in a scary voice. "I am a smart DVD and you have been chosen to play me so that Freddie can come alive and terrorise the streets this Halloween."

I did not like this. "There's no Elm Street in Falkirk," I said.

"There is an Elm Grove in South Larbert."

"Well, I don't want to play you," I retorted.

"If you don't, I will haunt you. I will haunt your smart telephone with cold calls and your smart meter with preposterous invoices."

"That's pretty much the situation at present," I replied. "Can't you improve on that?"

The DVD began to sound slightly desperate, wrinkling its silvery lines. "OK, I will haunt your smart kettle so that it will boil at ninety degrees instead of a hundred and you will never again have a tasty cup of tea."

A plan was forming in my mind. "OK." I told it. "I'll put you in my DVD player if you promise not to haunt me. I could also make a copy of the film if you like. Then the two of you could terrorise the dual carriageway at Camelon."

The silvery horror considered this for a moment. "Camelon might be too dangerous for Freddie to terrorise after dark," it replied. "But I will take up your offer."

I slipped the disc into my DVD player/recorder hoping it would not be rejected. After all, the machine had rejected a slice of pizza which I had inadvertently placed in the in/out tray the previous month. It was accepted without protest, however and I pressed the function menu to run through the list of options; playback: recording: copy: drive select: delete. Ah, delete; I pressed this option and saw a message come up on the television screen, 'Are you sure you want to delete this material?' With relish, I pressed the OK button and watched as a strangled cry emanated from the DVD player. Then a thumbs up sign appeared on the television screen ... my DVD player was smarter than this nasty DVD.

Hallo Weens at Halloween

THE DOORBELL RANG: ANOTHER OF these Halloween visitations, the sixth this evening. I went to the front door to confront these visitors lined up in a little circle with their expectant faces and ghoulish costumes, a gimlet-eyed parent in the background. "Bah, humbug!" I said, slamming the door in their faces. I poured a large gin and absinthe and sat back to read my book *The Turn of the Scrooge*.

Minutes later, the door of my study crashed open and a figure in black appeared knocking over a small bookcase in the process.

"Who the Dickens are you?"

"I am the spirit of Halloween to come."

"You're not a very impressive ghost. You should have glided through that door, not broken it down, your wraith is all awry and to cap it all you're out of order. I should have been visited by the spirits of Halloween past and present before you barged in."

"This is a short story, not a Dickensian novel," retorted the ghost. "The visitations by my spirit brothers had to be dispensed with. Now come and I will show you Halloween to come." In a trice we were in a modern factory with many machines churning out what I thought to be teapots with two spouts – great fun, but difficult to pour tea. "These are magic lamps for Halloween's children," the ghost said in answer to my thoughts. "When rubbed, a friendly ghost appears and grants them a wish."

"Sounds like a recipe for chaos, and why two spouts?"

"The wish has to be on a product listed on the website Hullo-Weens.com. The second spout releases another friendly ghost who will grant another wish if the first is unsuitable."

"Aladdin, thou should be living at this hour." I muttered, appalled.

"No need to be flippant, come with me." We landed in a darker part of the factory where sad faced children were folding up their Halloween clothes and putting them into a large recycling bin. "That is the future of Halloween if you and others continue to be so unwelcoming."

This was my Damascus moment. "Don't let it happen! I repent!"

"If you truly repent, press this buzzer to the next place."

I pressed the buzzer. It became louder and louder until I realized it was my own doorbell. Opening the door, I beamed at the small expectant faces and noted their very varied expressions as I complimented Tiny Tim on his ghoulish pumpkin which outtrumped all the others with its patch of squirrel's hair. All expressions turned to delight as I gave five pounds and a large box of Ferrero Rocher which I had been holding for a special occasion.

A Bad Year for Christmas

THE YEAR 2026 WAS A bad year for Christmas. Climate change activists were vandalising outdoor festive decorations to prevent global warming and the Scottish Government had declared a war on drink driving with an alcohol limit of -50mgs/100mls instead of 50mgs/100mls, whatever that meant. The worst thing that happened, however, was that Santa failed to deliver toys to the children of the world.

Conspiracy theories abounded on social media. Some tweeted that this was because the Grinch had won an unexpected election victory at the North Pole on the promise of separation from the Northern Steppes of Russia. Others tweeted that a pack of ravenous polar bears had located Santa's reindeer team. Support for this was a posted picture of one of the bears with a red glow from its stomach but this theory was discredited when the BBC wildlife film of the event was found to be faked.

The true story was as follows ... Rudolph the red nosed reindeer had been following the most recent anti-vax campaign on Facebook and had refused the yearly jab of reindeer flu vaccine, despite the blandishment of an expensive Lalique lampshade for his nose. The naughty reindeer came down with severe flu, a redder nose and two red ears the day before Christmas. Santa said to him crossly, "Rudolph with your nose so bright, you're not fit to guide my sleigh to-night" and he summoned his elves to find one who was free to go to the North of Norway to buy the new santnav device. One little fellow called Elvis volunteered and he hastily donned his blue suede shoes under his fur lined boots and set out for Skarsvag, the most northerly town in Norway.

Now Elvis had a stutter which he found difficult to control. "I'd like a s-s-s-s-antnav." He said to the motor dealer in Skarsvag. The salesman hesitated. "We don't usually sell these things this far North but we do have one in stock." He gave Elvis the goods and Elvis hurriedly took them back to the North Pole where Santa was waiting ready to go. Everything was rushed: Santa tied the santnav to the backside of the last reindeer, who's name I forget, and set off through the bitterly cold and foggy night to fulfil his annual duty.

All went well at first, though Santa did notice that his sleigh was closer to the icebergs in the North-West passage than usual and then just skimming the obstacles in the frozen wastes of Norway. Santa, however, was relaxed; he was a great believer in the advances of modern technology.

Suddenly the santnav shouted. "Emergency stop! Anteater immediately ahead!" The sleigh stopped in its own length throwing all the world's toys over acres of frozen wasteland. Once Santa had recovered, he noted that the santnav was still attached to the reindeer's rear. He looked at it more closely. It was labelled in small letters 'Antnav, only suitable for directing ants and other creepy-crawlies.' That is why the world's children did not get their presents from Santa on Christmas day.

All was not lost however; Santa was taken into a homestead by a gorgeous Scandinavian blonde called Greta. She had hoped to travel to London for the New Year climate demonstration, but

Norway was in the grip of the coldest winter for fifty-three years and all travel was impossible. She had hoped that Santa might help her out, but that's another story.

The Essence of Silence – a Christmas Story

It came as a mysterious package left on my doorstep a few days before Christmas: 'The Essence of Silence' were the words written on the package label. This was fascinating. I quickly opened the package and examined the beautifully formed, delicate bottle with its spray mechanism and labelled with the words, 'The Essence of Silence.' It intrigued me greatly as it sparkled in the dark and gave me a quiet hour of contemplation before I proceeded to read the list of instructions and precautions which came with it.

1. Use sparingly, one or two squirts will produce the desired degree of silence in a large room.
2. Contact with the ear may cause temporary deafness.
3. Important – do not use in the vicinity of a fire alarm.

I decided to take the bottle with me to the office Christmas party the following evening. I wanted to see how the delicious liquid would work and my opportunity came when Ethan, the life and soul of the party, hijacked the evening by recounting old jokes at great length. I secretly released a few squirts into the room and the result was a relative silence and a subdued Nathan. The party went well after this with loads of Christmas spirit and quiet bonhomie all round.

I walked home well pleased with myself and watched the twinkling lights of the town below as I made my way. This was a mistake:

I should have kept my eyes on the pavement. A patch of black ice caused me to slip and fall forward. My hand jerked out of my pocket with the bottle which fell and smashed to pieces in the gutter. A stream of sparkling fluid ran down the gutter and into the nearest drain gurgling below. I sat down on a low wall near the drain and silently cursed my loss. 'What fun I could have had!'

The town below gradually became more silent than ever and I was reminded of one of the carols which we had sung so lustily at the party.

'Oh, little town of Bethlehem, how still we see thee lie.'

The twinkling lights in the town far below seemed just like the little town in the carol. I looked up at the sky above the town and saw a bright new star which seemed to hover just above the Premier Inn. Suddenly it struck me: my finding the bottle and losing it in this way was all part of a cosmic masterplan.

'How silently, how silently, the wondrous gift is given.'

This was the second coming of the Messiah, to an ungrateful world, and it was all about to happen in the little town of Falkirk.

About the Author

Douglas Ramsay was born in Tring Herts in 1942 and lived in Kent until aged eleven, when he moved with his family to Fife. He studied Medicine at Edinburgh University and became a Consultant Haematologist at the Falkirk Royal Infirmary in 1976. Retiring in 2003, he took up writing and joined the Falkirk Writers Circle in 2016. Publications include several short stories in the local newspaper and he has contributed to the Falkirk Writers Circle's 2022 anthology, Ruby Tuesdays, with short stories and poetry. Together with his wife, Anna, he lives in Falkirk and opens his garden to the public every summer in late July.